for Viggo!

— Kevin

KEVAN ATTEBERRY

Ghost Cat

NEAL PORTER BOOKS

HOLIDAY HOUSE / NEW YORK

For the ghosts in my life

Neal Porter Books

Text and illustrations copyright © 2019 by Kevan Atteberry

All Rights Reserved

HOLIDAY HOUSE is registered in the U.S. Patent and Trademark Office.

Printed and bound in October 2018 at Toppan Leefung, DongGuan City, China.

The artwork for this book was made using digital tools.

Book design by Jennifer Browne

www.holidayhouse.com

First Edition

1   3   5   7   9   10   8   6   4   2

Library of Congress Cataloging-in-Publication Data

Names: Atteberry, Kevan, author, illustrator.

Title: Ghost cat / Kevan Atteberry.

Description: First edition. | New York : Holiday House, [2019] | "Neal Porter

Books." | Summary: A boy who used to have a cat believes that its ghost is

darting through his house by day and purring in his bed at night.

Identifiers: LCCN 2018028289 | ISBN 9780823442836 (hardcover)

Subjects: | CYAC: Ghosts—Fiction. | Cats—Fiction.

Classification: LCC PZ7.A866395 Gho 2019 | DDC [E]—dc23 LC record available

at https://lccn.loc.gov/2018028289

There is a ghost in my house.

I've only seen it out of
the corner of my eye,
but I think it's a cat.

I know because I used to have one.

There's a dash from
the left, or a dart
from the right.

It's always gone before
I can really see it.

Sometimes I hear it.

Sometimes I feel it.

But mostly it's a quick, dark blur. Here, and then not here.

Often at night
I feel its weight,
its warmth,
its purring.

When I look,
it's gone.

Today I heard it
mewing at my
bedroom door.

I was too slow
to catch it.

I heard the jangle of a cat toy
bouncing down the stairs.

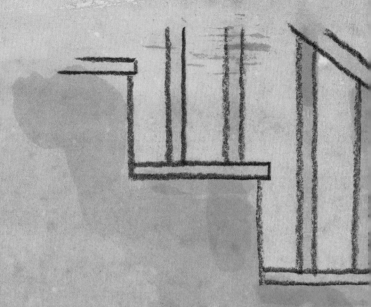

I heard a thud
in the den.

A crash in the kitchen.

A splash in the living room.

Then finally
I saw it.

And followed it . . .

. . . to where it sat
by the door, staring
at me, purring, like
my cat used to do
when it wanted
to go out.

After a few moments . . .

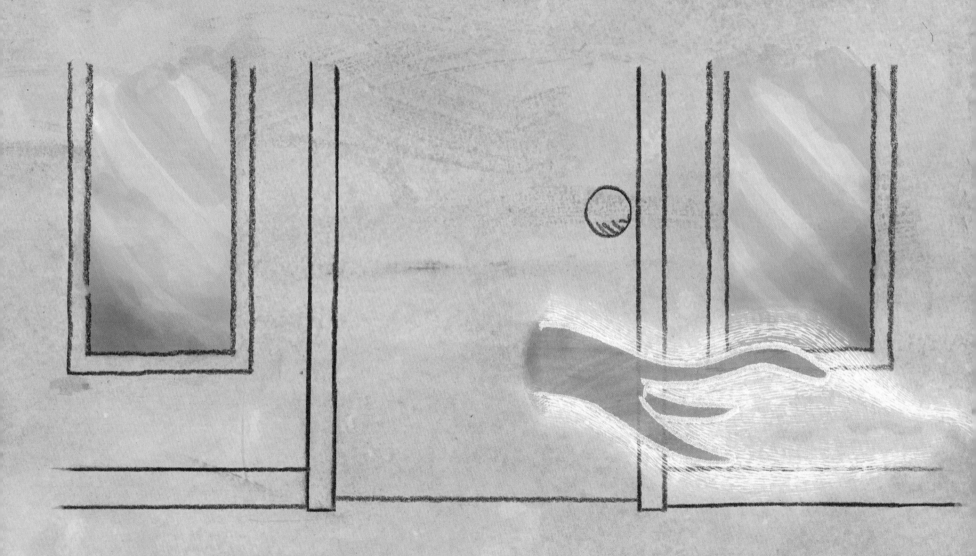

. . . it turned and leapt right through the door.

When I opened it . . .

. . . I found you.

There is a ghost
in our house.